the Tortoise
and the
Hare

templar publishing

nahta nój

Once upon a time, there lived
a **brash** and **boastful**
hare and an *old* and
humble tortoise.

Early one morning, the hare announced:
"I am the **fastest** in the forest.
I challenge anyone to beat me in a race!"

"I will race you," said Tortoise.

"YOU?" exclaimed Hare.
"Ridiculous! You are much
too old and slow."

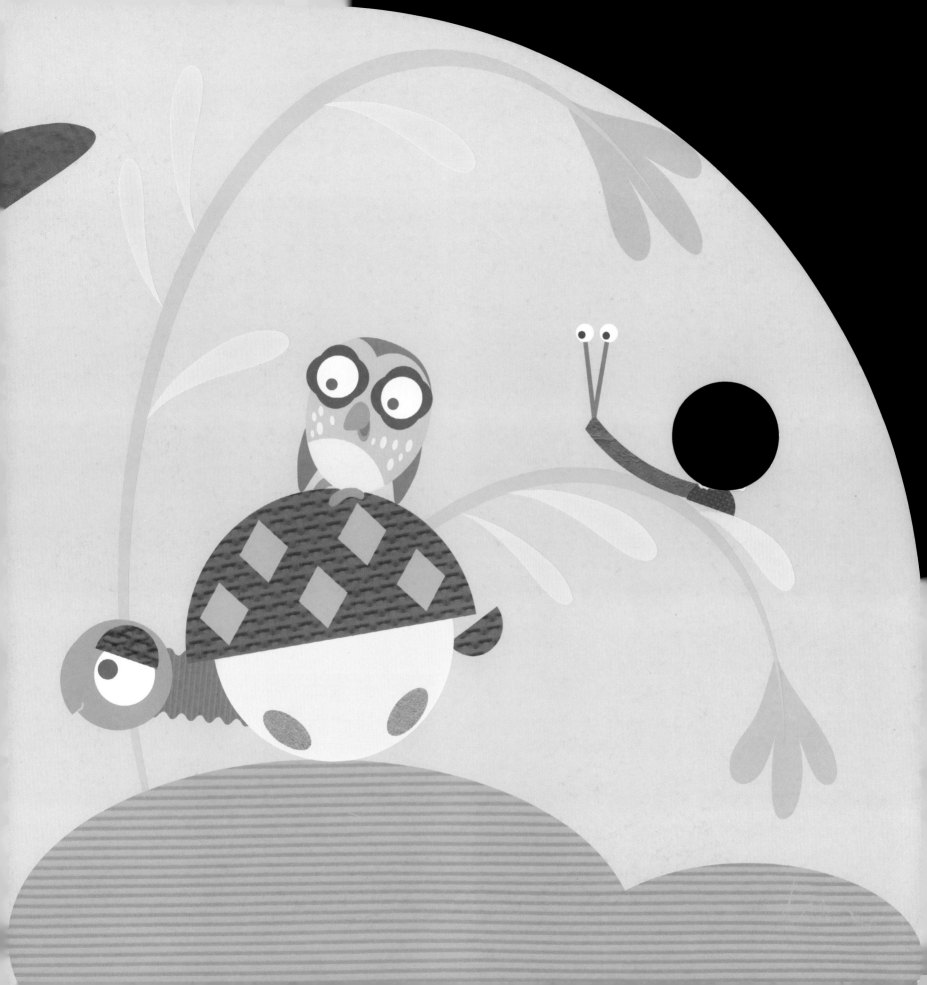

"Remember, Hare," Wise Owl said, "pride comes before a *fall*."

Hare laughed, but he agreed to race Tortoise.

Owl set the course.

It was twisty ...

START

END

and very . . .

very **long!**

and turny . . .

"Ready, set, **GO!**" he shouted.

He sped around a tree stump . . .

Hare **bounded** off.

hopped
over a log . . .

leapt across a puddle.

Soon Tortoise was just a speck in the distance.

Ha! thought Hare. *That'll teach him to think he's as fast as me.*

And, feeling peckish, he stopped to snack on some grass.

Then Hare began to feel sleepy.
I'll just have a quick nap, he thought.
That tortoise will never catch up.

zzzzzzz

But as soon as he lay down, he fell into a deep sleep.

z z z Z Z Z Z

Meanwhile, Tortoise kept **plodding** on . . .

and on.

Soon, the end was in sight!

END

As the sun began to set,
Hare woke up, startled.

"The **RACE!**" he gasped.

He **ran** as fast as he could to the finish line . . .

But Tortoise was **already there!**

Tortoise had

WON

the
race!

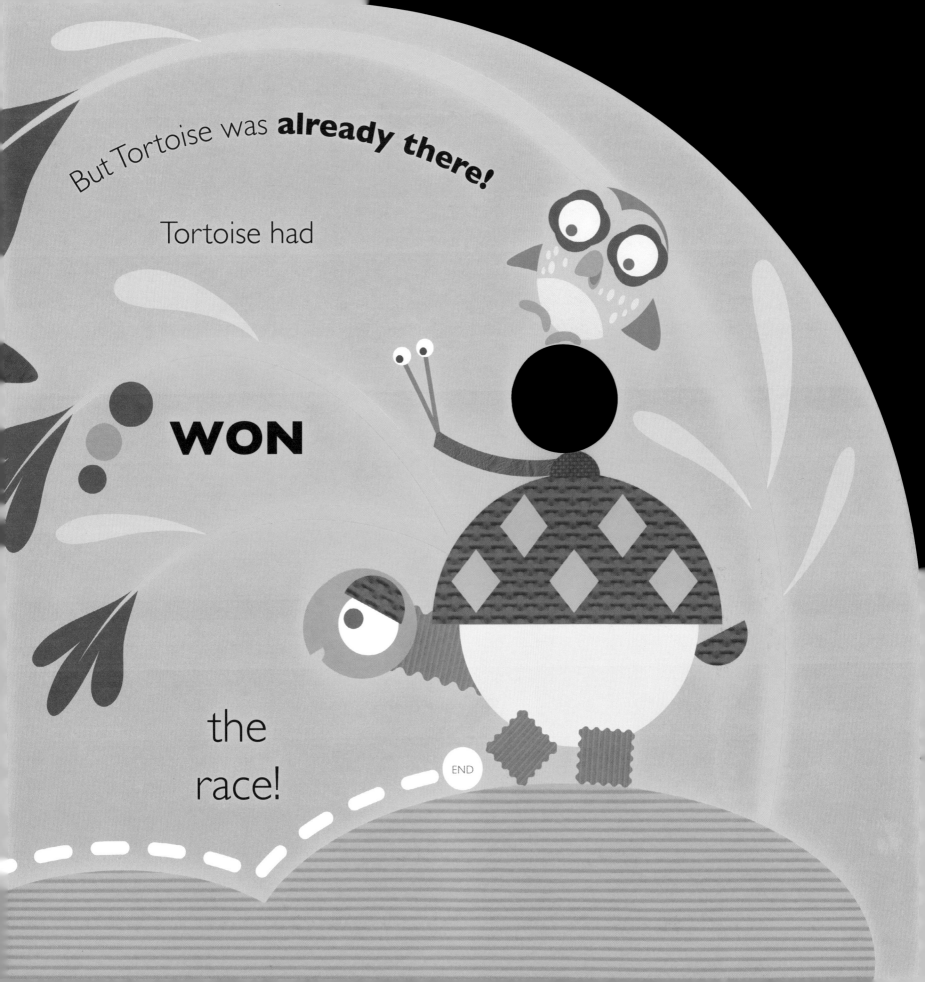

END

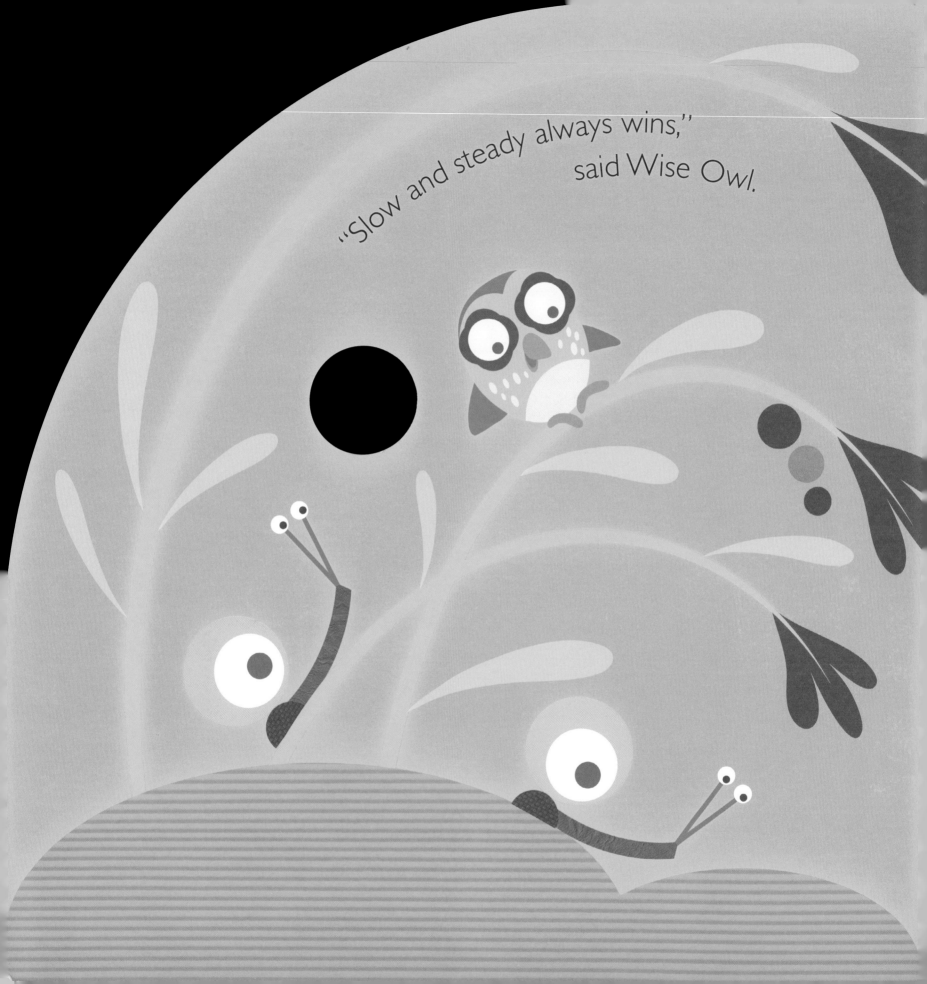

Hare felt ashamed of being so **brash** and **boastful**, and from that day on,

he **never** made fun of anybody again.

A TEMPLAR BOOK

First published in the UK in paperback in 2015 by Templar Publishing,
an imprint of The Templar Company Limited,
Deepdene Lodge, Deepdene Avenue, Dorking,
Surrey, RH5 4AT, UK

www.templarco.co.uk

ISBN 978-1-78370-178-0

Retold by Alison Ritchie
Illustrated by Nahta Nój
Designed by Jonathan Lambert

Printed in China

For Loulou and Elle,
my inspiration and energy – N. N.